Disney

Cinderella

A Dream Is a Wish Your Heart Makes

Lyrics by Al Hoffman, Jerry Livingston, and Mack David

Illustrated by Gabby Zapata

A GOLDEN BOOK • NEW YORK

A Dream Is a Wish Your Heart Makes
Words and Music by Al Hoffman, Jerry Livingston, and Mack David
 Published in the United States by Golden Books, an imprint of Random House Children's Books, a division of Penguin Random House LLC, 1745 Broadway, New York, NY 10019, and in Canada by Penguin Random House Canada Limited, Toronto, in conjunction with Disney Enterprises, Inc. Golden Books, A Golden Book, A Little Golden Book, the G colophon, and the distinctive gold spine are registered trademarks of Penguin Random House LLC.
rhcbooks.com
ISBN 978-0-7364-4513-9 (trade) — ISBN 978-0-7364-4514-6 (ebook)
Printed in the United States of America
10 9 8 7 6 5 4 3 2 1

A dream . . .

is a wish

your heart makes

when you're fast asleep.

In dreams, you will lose your heartaches.

Whatever you wish for,

you keep.

Have faith in your

dreams, and someday

your rainbow will

come smiling through.

No matter how your heart is grieving,

if you keep on believing,

the dream that you wish . . .

will come true.

And they lived happily
ever after!